P9-ASF-842

The World Is Big and I'm So Small

by WILLIAM KOTZWINKLE

pictures by JOE SERVELLO

Crown Publishers, Inc. NEW YORK

OCT 1986

JEFFERSONVILLE TOWNSHIP PUBLIC LIBRARY
JEFFERSONVILLE INDIANA

j
e
K876w

Text copyright © 1986 by William Kotzwinkle
Illustrations copyright © 1986 by Joe Servello

All rights reserved.
No part of this book may be reproduced or transmitted
in any form or by any means,
electronic or mechanical, including photocopying,
recording, or by any information storage and retrieval system,
without permission in writing from the publisher.

Published by Crown Publishers Inc.,
225 Park Avenue South, New York, New York 10003,
and represented in Canada by the Canadian Manda Group

CROWN is a trademark of Crown Publishers, Inc.

Manufactured in Japan

Library of Congress Cataloging-in-Publication Data

Kotzwinkle, William. The world is big and I'm so small.
Summary: Rhymed text and illustrations describe
the activities of a very young rabbit from getting up
in the morning to going to bed at night.
[1. Stories in rhyme. 2. Rabbits—Fiction]
I. Servello, Joe, ill. II. Title.
PZ8.3.K8533Wo 1986 [E] 86-4560
ISBN 0-517-56310-X
Design by Jane Byers Bierhorst
10 9 8 7 6 5 4 3 2 1
First Edition

8607433

"It's morning," said the bird
who could not fly.
"Don't you wish," said the fish,
"we could swim through the sky?"

The water said, "I'll wash the sleep out of your head."

The high chair sighed. "He takes me for an awful ride."

The pots, they all went tumbling down,
except for one, which was a crown.

Why don't I give this room a try?

"Hello, I'm here, who's that, good-bye."

I like to help whenever I can
because I am the laundry man!

The world is big and I'm so small.

I'd better eat and grow up tall!

...and the knights came riding to the hall.

"I'm leaving home to be a knight."

"Forward march, let's go, left…right…"

Dig, dig, dig, in the nice soft ground.

What is that? Do you hear a sound?

"Here comes the King!" the knights did cry.

And sure enough, the King came by.

"Daddy, let me see. Daddy, read to me.
Daddy, let me on your knee."

"Eat your carrots and we'll go for a ride."

"Away we go, up the mountainside!"

"It's nighttime," said the bird,
"and we'll be sleeping soon."
"Don't you wish," said the fish,
"we could swim to the moon?"